# THE GAME OF YOUR LIFE

# GAME
# OF
# YOUR
# LIFE

Genre: Sci-Fic Mystery

Author: Minister Larry Montgomery, Sr.
montgomerybusiness@hotmail.com

1

# THE GAME OF YOUR LIFE

# GAME OF YOUR LIFE

## Genre: Sci-Fic Mystery

If you think Video Game Playing is the way of the future then this story is for you. Here we take a hard look at that dream job in the future. In the year 2050, today's Video Game Playing dream job becomes a real life nightmare since you literally have to risk your life to collect your paycheck.

Follow Randy Hatchfield a year 2050 video game quality assurance agent who sets out to collect the biggest paycheck of his career, from an employer who will stop at nothing to keep him from collecting it. Randy like you or I, has followed the rules, put in his hours, and is now ready to get paid. Follow him through the longest 24 hours of his life and see what it costs him to collect the biggest paycheck of his life in the 'GAME OF YOUR LIFE.'

Author: Minister Larry Montgomery, Sr.
Baldwin, New York 11510
montgomerybusiness@hotmail.com

# THE GAME OF YOUR LIFE

## ABOUT THIS BOOK

In the year 2050 Reality TV is the only kind of television available. The broadcast and television industry is now built on total access. Television shows no longer have time limits any show can air 24 hours a day, 7 days a week, 12 months a year. It is a time when Cable television, Direct TV and Dish television providers are no longer limited to specific video or satellite sources as conduits to providing access to programming. They can access any and all public video feeds, municipal video networks, private security networks, digital camera feeds or even personal wireless connections in an effort to accommodate subscriber demands. Any and everything can be accessed at any time, and or anywhere if you have the right subscriber package. Any citizen's life can become the next great fade and be put on a public or private broadcast network just by clicking on their image.

Total access to your life in real time is only limited by the viewing package the subscriber ordered. There are three types of packages: Basic, Special and Premium. If you have a Basic Subscriber Package you can watch anyone, anywhere, at anytime as long as they are in a public place. The Special Subscriber Package allows subscribers to see everything in the Basic Subscriber Package plus it gives access into a person's personal space such as their home, office or backyard. Only the Premium Subscriber Package allows total access. The Premium Subscriber service includes roaming access, it allows you to watch anyone, anywhere at anytime even in their bedrooms and bathrooms; as long as there is a camera in the area. Roaming access allows the subscriber to access video feeds from traffic camera's, security camera's, webcam's, iPad's, and iPhone's, if they are in close enough proximity to the viewing subject. Anyone of these portals can be used to access and provide video feeds, because in the year 2050, it is a time when access to any electronic, digital or wireless device cannot be denied to Premium Package Subscribers by law.

At this point in time there is literally no privacy from Premium Package subscribers, all they need do is pick a person, any person, from anyplace (i.e.: the middle of Times Square on New Years Eve) and  click on their image, and they will get their Personal Channel Number (PCN).

# THE GAME OF YOUR LIFE

By using someone's PCN a subscriber can follow them around wherever they go for as long as they want. Premium Package Subscribers can watch any person's, whole life unfold, in real time.

Our story focuses on several Premium Package subscribers, all from different walks of life, who have become bored with the latest national video fade; stealing Mega Lottery tickets. The goal of this national pastime is to identify prospective Mega Lottery winners. Then watch them to see where the winners hide their winning ticket prior to redeeming them; so they can steal it. A major lottery prize winning ticket may go through several hands before it is redeemed which makes for very exciting television.

Recently many Premium Package Subscribers have turned their attention to the second fastest growing national pastime known as testing video games for dollars.

Video game testing for dollars, offers two distinct opportunities to earn dollars. First; anyone interested must sign up and be qualified. With their application they get free first release video games to test, rate, score and critique. Doing this, they can earn upwards of $100.00 per hour, just for playing video games the dream job of the 22nd century. There is no limit to the number of games a member can play or the number of hours they can play them, the whole process is computerized. These testers are called Quality Assurance Agents (QA's).

To qualify for the no limit game testing earnings, the prospective QA'er must have checked the 'Full Experience Agent Box' on their application. When that box is checked on the application two things happen: first; the applicant is automatically signed up for the Ultimate Insider Game –'The Game of your Life.'

Secondly the prospective QA'er gives the gaming company permission to include itself as a beneficiary on any and all of the QA'ers personal life insurance policies, as well as authorization to open as many short term life insurance policy's in their name as they please. The gaming company usually designates itself as beneficiary on policies in amounts of $250,000.00, or more for periods of 33 days at a time.

In exchange, during that 33 day period, the QA'er has full access to all of the company's computer games as well as open access to the list of other QA'ers who become eligible to play the Game of your Life.

# THE GAME OF YOUR LIFE

While Full Access QA'ers can earn upwards of $100.00 per hour, just for testing the games, the maximum total earnings opportunity for each 32 day period is $76,800.00, tax free.

Now that the stage is set, we can talk about the challenge: Getting paid. In order to get paid, any amount over, what the company determines is a satisfactory 32 day testing workload, you are automatically placed on the Game of your Life players list-- whether you want to play it or not.

Every Game of Your Life player must come to the gaming company's Claims Office to be paid on the 33 day. If you want to be paid you must bring your claim voucher receipt to the Claims office no earlier than the beginning of the 33$^{rd}$ day and no later than the end of the 33$^{rd}$ day. That means you only have a 24 hour window to claim your earnings.

The gaming company's standing policy is, 'any QA'er who stops any player on the Game of Your Life participants list, from collecting their earnings, can earn upwards of $5,000.00 over and above their own 32 day testing Claim and bonus dollars as well.

Now let the game begin…Randy Hatchfield is a seasoned video game tester who has never attempted to collect the big Claim money. Randy always settles for the designated monthly workload payout even though there were many months when he personally had gone over. This time things are different. This time Randy can't afford to accept less than he has earned. Earlier this month Randy learned that he has corporal tunnel syndrome the result of hours of constant use from operating his video game console; and he is only 35 years of age. After that Randy made up his mind to weather as many sleepless nights as necessary to earn the big 32 day game playing Claim fee, and then collect it.

This story is about Randy's quest to collect the biggest prize the Game of Your Life had to offer, but what will it cost him?

# THE GAME OF YOUR LIFE

ISBN: 978-0-9836919-8-3
Published by Emerging Business Group, Inc.
Baldwin, New York.

# THE GAME OF YOUR LIFE

Dedicated to my wife Joyous
and my children for their love and support.

# THE GAME OF YOUR LIFE

## ABOUT THE AUTHOR

Minister Larry Montgomery, Sr., is a retired Commercial Bank Vice President currently Chief Editor and Publisher of the only weekly African-American community newspaper in Nassau County, Long Island, New York.

Minister Larry Montgomery, Sr. earned his MBA from Hofstra University in Hempstead, New York where he grew up, married his wife Joyous Reynolds of 40 years and raised three loving children: Larry Jr., William Lamont, and April Nicole.

As a member of Glory Temple Ministries, Inc., under the Pastorship of Senior Pastor Apostle Ronnie Deadwyler and Co-Pastor Apostle Dr. Karen Deadwyler, who in obedience to the Father, planted the seed of "Scribe" on Minister Montgomery's heart. To that end, Minister Montgomery committed to penning twelve of the Lord's parables under the cover of the life and times of a fictional character by the name of Harry Bailey, a U.S. Marshal.

This is Minister Montgomery's second project; the first being the twelve book fictional series of crime and investigative adaptations from selected biblical parables, including the "Persistent Widow," as taken from Luke 8: 1-5 KJV, in the above mentioned series U.S. Marshal Harry Bailey and the Parables of Life Series.

While the events of the story may seem familiar, they are merely examples of how the hand of God may be working in each of our daily lives. Yes, there are a few, and only a few of our more spicy everyday words in the body of this and those works, but none of the more radical and down right offensive ones will be found in it.

I hope that you enjoy the readings, and that you might find an idea or two in each, and possibly some new information or revelation about something or some place found in them.

# THE GAME OF YOUR LIFE

Thank you for considering this work and please feel free to pass it on. I hope you find a few moments of relaxation from reading any of these books and that you look forward to reading the complete twelve book series of biblical adaptations in the Parables of Life series as well as this second project 'The game of Your Life' and look forward to our upcoming series "City of Prophecy". The City of Prophesy series is scheduled to roll out late 2013, God willing.

May God continue to Bless You and Yours!

# THE GAME OF YOUR LIFE

## TABLE OF CONTENTS

See a list of our other projects on Page 108

# THE GAME OF YOUR LIFE

## CHAPTER 1

# BEFORE BREAKFAST

The time clock stamped 7:00am on William Stones time card with a loud slamming sound, louder than ever before which made him turn to Tommie the Security Guard and say, "I thought you were going to have someone fix that thing?" Tommie looked up from his desk and said, "I did tell someone to fix it and they haven't come around to get it done yet… Oh! Wait a minute here he is right now…it was you!" Both of the men laughed out loud. Then William started towards the main lobby maintenance closet looking out the massive 30 foot high windows at the crowd of people waiting online to turn in their Claims vouchers upstairs at Global Video Game Developers.

As William walked away he said to Tommie, "It looks as if its gonna be another busy day for you, man!" Tommie stood up and started to walk towards the front doors and said, "It's the 33rd day. It's always crazy down here. People trying to get paid, people trying to keep other people from being paid, so they can get paid.

11

# THE GAME OF YOUR LIFE

And people trying to get paid from people who are trying to get paid from people who are trying to keep other people from getting paid. It's a vicious cycle but at least everyone is working at getting paid."

William stopped suddenly and turned and said to Tommie, what are we going to do when it is time to retire?"

Tommie stopped and said, "Retire? Retire! Who can afford to retire? I'm hoping that I die no earlier than 1 hour after I get my weekly check and no later than one hour before I have to return to work the next week. What's your plan?"

William smiled and said, "Well my plan is to retire from here and get 80% of my salary, then get a part time job working here and earn 20% of my salary so I can continue to live the same life style but only work half as hard for a while. Then I'll spend half of my day working here, inside and the other half of my day standing on the other side of those windows online outside, so once a month I can collect a few dollars for video game testing. The rest of my time will be spent trying to catch one of those 'Game of Your Life' players so I can take their claim voucher just like the other fools on line out there."

# THE GAME OF YOUR LIFE

Tommie smiled and said, "Now that sounds like a retirement plan" and he laughed and walked away.

William hurried to get his day started, as usual he planned to start cleaning the 32$^{nd}$ floor Penthouse Offices first and then work his way down to the 31$^{st}$ floor by mid afternoon.

In the elevator on his way up to the penthouse, William listened to the Global Video Games Developers standard Claims Office disclaimer, for what seemed to be the millionth time. He listens to this disclaimer every time he takes the express elevator from the lobby to the penthouse suite on the 33rd floor. Although William usually drowns out the commercial by turning up his MP3 player he forgot this morning so he just had no choice but to listen today.

The Announcer said, "Are you tired of the day to day grind? Do you love to play video games? Wouldn't you like to take it easy and get paid to relax at home?

If you answered 'yes' to these three questions then you could qualify for the highly lucrative position as Video Game Quality Assurance Agent or Game Tester. As a Quality Assurance Agent or Video Game Tester you can earn upwards of $100.00 per hour just for playing any of our video games and then preparing a personal satisfaction report.

When you join Global Video Game Developers Quality Assurance or Video Game Tester Teams you will receive unlimited access to all of our upcoming new releases. You can examine each of them as much as you

13

want as often as you want. You will also be immediately entered in to the fastest growing reality television show in the history of television, 'the Game of your life.' And you will receive access to our Premium digital, wireless or cable television subscriber service to further enhance your 'Game of Your Life' viewing and participation experience.

Remember; to qualify for no limit game testing earnings, you must check the 'Full Experience Agent Box' on your application which allows your inclusion in our 33$^{rd}$ voucher and playing cycle.

Once you have completed your application and been approved you can start earning while you play. Just stop by our Claims Office anytime during the 33$^{rd}$ day of your game playing cycle to be paid. Remember to ask about our bonus dollars opportunity when you submit your earnings cycle payment voucher. It's that easy and welcome aboard."

As soon as the commercial ended the elevator stopped and the doors opened to the penthouse lobby where William got off and went to the Janitors closet to prepare for the workday ahead.

Downstairs in the Lobby

Just as William stepped off the elevator all hell broke loose in front of the building when not one, not two but three bodies fell from the penthouse roof onto the sidewalk in front of the building, hitting several of the people on the Claims Office line.

As soon as Tommie saw the crowd start to break and run he noticed three separate shower spray-like streams

14

# THE GAME OF YOUR LIFE

of blood splatter running down the fronts of the buildings 30 foot high lobby windows.

Tommie quickly pulled out his NexTel and chirped a code red, then he walked over to the electrical box to make sure that none of the lobby doors were still on automatic open for 9:00am. He knew to turn all lobby entrance locks to manual operation during times of public distress and waited for the police to come and take charge.

It was not unusual for a certain amount of physical altercations to take place in front of the office building, particularly at the end of the 32 day cycle; the 33$^{rd}$ day, when every one shows up to get paid. If it wasn't for the buildings separate entrance to the Claims Office, Tommie's guard post would need between six to eight more men to assure some kind of order on Claims Day.

The time was 8:10am, and based on past experience, Tommie knew it wouldn't take the police more than 4 minutes from being called to actually showing up.

Tommie waited and watched the crowd act like a gaggle of geese flocking around and chattering at one another as if to identify who to blame over what had just happened. Then, like clockwork, phase two kicked

# THE GAME OF YOUR LIFE

in. The crowd turned into a pack of wolves. Clawing and tearing at each other as the closet few tried to pick the pockets of the dead trio to find their Claim voucher receipts.

This time it was particularly ugly as Tommie explained to the lead officer of the squad of officers that had just arrived.

A van load of plain cloth detectives showed up right on time, and immediately behind them was a squad of uniformed officers dressed in full riot gear in the back of a SWAT bus. Detective Douglas Thompson was the lead detective assigned to this investigation and he was the first of a two man team that came into the lobby area to take Tommie's statement. But before Tommie could rattle off the standard corporate response he heard the other detective say, "You know there must be a way to get this company to change the way it does business. I mean we are here damn near every 33 days like clock work." Det. Thompson smiled and said, "Don't waste your breath; it would take an act of Congress to change the law to stop this kind of employer created violence. The economy is so bad that any conversation concerning changes in claims practices or policies will almost always lead to riots. So don't go there. Let's just

# THE GAME OF YOUR LIFE

do the job, by the numbers and get the hell up out of here…"

Tommie thought to himself: "Up until the company started offering that bonus dollar program there was a lot less violence on Claims day…" Then Tommie gave the detectives the usual corporate disclaimer and they went up to the building management's office to examine the roof top security tape.

7:00am Randy Hatchfield's Home

Randy's eyes slowly opened as the thick night shades that covered his bedroom window rose to the beat of the song 'Money, Money, Money' by the O'Jays 1970's hit single.

Randy's 4T touch phone named '40G' had already started the official NY Mets espresso and latte making machine as scheduled and turned on the hot water nozzle in the shower.

As the bright skinned, 6'4" former high school lacrosse player put his size 13's into his Huckleberry Hound shaped fuzzy slippers and tied on his George Jetson bathrobe he yawned and rubbed his two day old

# THE GAME OF YOUR LIFE

stumble and said, "40G today's the day and there is no stopping us now."

The now 20 year old hand held electronic phone and personal assistant flashed and pumped up the volume of the song to a fever pitch and then settled down to the designated room volume.

This morning was a special morning for Randy, it was the 33$^{rd}$ day of the video gaming quality assurance agents pay cycle and he had decided the prior evening to claim the full number of game playing hours he played for the last 32 days. At the end of the last cycle Randy had logged in almost 380 hours, just under 12 hours a day, playing his favorite video game, "The Game of Your Life." Randy realized if he had claimed the full value of his efforts he would have been eligible to collect $38,000.00 tax free. But he would have been automatically entered into the very game he loved to play, for real, since that month's threshold was only $3,500.00.

This had been the case for the last 8 years, Randy was to afraid of what the other game players, turned bounty hunters, would have done to him for the $5,000.00 reward they would have gotten for stopping him from collecting his $38,000.00, plus whatever their video

# THE GAME OF YOUR LIFE

game playing dollars they were entitled to for the same month.

But this months Claim would be different. This month Randy can't afford to accept less than he has worked so hard to earn. This month he is going for the big money. He has clocked almost 700 hours of game playing time and he has calculated that at a rate of $100.00 per hour, it entitles him to $70,000.00. Just enough to cover his first installment on his retirement annuity, which after 10 years will pay him $5,000.00 a month for life after retirement. Randy now a 35 year old, under educated, video game quality assurance agent, was just told that he is showing early signs of corporal tunnel syndrome in both hands. So it would seem as though his career as a professional video game tester is coming to a slow and painful end. Without any other discernible skills, in a society without social security or even welfare benefits, men like Randy are looking at financial ruin before age 40 and who knows what after that.

Public Law 100-18B clearly states: no job, no income you're considered a vagrant and subject to incarceration in a federal penitentiary until such time as your situation changes.

# THE GAME OF YOUR LIFE

Finding out that information forced Randy to finally make up his mind and go for the full value claim and take on the "The Game of Your Life."

Seated in his favorite white form fitting plastic kitchen table chair which sits under a round glass kitchen table top in his 1950's retro style roadside diner kitchen in the rear of his 2 bedroom cape style home: Randy began to review the day's big claim, payday, plan with 40G.

Holding 40G up as if a handheld microphone Randy said, "40G open file 'Game of Your Life'." Almost five full seconds later 40G responded and said, "File available."

Randy responded as he pointed the project digital screen over the bouquet of artificial flowers that sat in the middle of the kitchen table and said, "Status!" 40G responded and said, "Fully charged and awaiting command."

Randy smiled and said, "Nice try 40G but you are moving very slow this morning should I recharge you?" 40G responded and said, "That does not compute." Randy smiled again and said, "Whatever…display audio and video files for subject command."

# THE GAME OF YOUR LIFE

Immediately a 3D replica of Randy standing in his bedroom displayed and started to speak.

"…Note to self, I will need to wear my all terrain converses, a pair of clean white indoor/outdoor calf high socks, my swimming trunks, my cargo pants, my mess under armor tee shirt with shell, I want to wear my Boy Scout explorer watch and carry my utility knife, gas mask and 3 stun guns. I'll need my crew neck body shirt over my under armor shell and a pair of leather biker gloves, sunglasses, afro wig, and 2015 Mets World Series baseball cap…"

"…I'll need to take my go-back-pack. Note to self, don't forget to check the go-back-pack and make sure that the following items are in it…"

Randy continued and said, "Pause file" and then he went into the guest bedroom which had been converted into a clothes closet, and looked for his go-back-pack and brought it back down to the kitchen. He sat it down on one of the other kitchen chairs and began to go through it.

As he unzipped the backpack he said, "Resume."
"…solar flashlight, 2 light sticks, solar battery charger,

# THE GAME OF YOUR LIFE

dog whistle, touch phone, small vanishing blanket, lighter, 10' para cord, dust mask, $500 in emergency cash –2 $100 dollar bills, 2 $50's and $200 dollars in singles, first aid kit, permanent black marker, waterproof paper and tape, identification card, ice pick, seltzer capsules, 4 pairs of handcuffs, 2 baggies of powdered strychnine, 6 Dixie cups, roll of 4 inch thick black tape, 4 M-80 firecrackers, pair of inline roller skates and a 36" x 24" cardboard sign that read, 'We want more hours'…"

When he finished checking the go-back-pack, Randy realized there were three more steps that had to be completed before he was ready to begin his quest; he needed to make sure he had the most important thing on his person, his Claim Voucher receipt with pin number. So he turned to 40G and said, "Remind me to validate my Claim as soon as I finish my shower and get dressed." 40G responded and said, "Task noted."

Each 32 day cycle claim voucher has to be pre-approved for processing and upon approval a pin I.D. number is forwarded via email to the claimant. The 16 digit pin number is the only way to verify that the claim should be paid to the person presenting it. The email carrying the validated claim voucher pin number also includes a link to the Claim Validation web page. On

# THE GAME OF YOUR LIFE

the Claim Validation web page is the Claimant submission amount based on hours logged for the cycle. And the cumulated missed validated claim amounts for the period.

It also provides the claimant their final opportunity to change their claim to an amount other than actually logged if they would prefer not to be entered into the 'Game of Your Life.' Once the claim amount is validated and if that amount is above the monthly threshold the claimant is automatically entered into the real time version of the "Game of Your Life." Where the grand prize includes the amount you've claimed for the past 32 day video game testing cycle, along with a grand prize that would include the collective amount of missed, game, claim vouchers for the prior gaming period and as a bonus, any claim dollars you accumulate for other claimants who will not make the claims Office themselves during the 24 hour claim window.

Bonus dollars are literally the accumulation of all claim vouchers you take off of anyone who attempts to stop you from presenting your valid claim that are also due on the day your claim is valid for.

# THE GAME OF YOUR LIFE

Then he needed to review his route to the Claims Office and lastly his plan for approaching the Claims Clerk Office to submit his claim.

Randy then commanded 40G to display his route to the Claims Office and send the file to his upstairs office printer and print 2 copies. As the route was being printed Randy attempted to commit it to memory.

The Route

Randy planned to drive his car... The distance from his home at 456 Oval Dr. to Global Video Game Development Claims Office was approximately 10 miles.

The quickest route was to take the 12 block drive along Oval Dr. to Lake Dr then make a right onto Walsingham Road -- I-688. Then take that approximately 6 1/4 miles veering left onto Ulmerton Road about another 5 miles. Make a left onto 130th Avenue North and go 6 blocks, look for 125th St. then make a right onto 125th Drive go another 10 blocks to 134th Ave. and make a right. Finally; travel 8 more blocks make a left into the parking lot of Global Video Game Development Claims Office Complex and then park.

# THE GAME OF YOUR LIFE

The drive to the Claims Office was estimated to take no longer than 30 minutes. The more time consuming challenge would be getting into the Global building and up to the Claims Office without major incident; which Randy knew, after playing the virtual video game and watching the reality show, the Game of Your Life would be the most daunting.

The game he has so reluctantly avoided for almost 8 years, but today was the day that all of that would change forever.

The video feed was suddenly interrupted and 40G said, "The printer has completed your request, would you like to review the attached notes?"

Randy responded and said, "Yes pull up my plans for entering the Claims Office."

Plans for Entering the Claims Office
Randy's plan for approaching the Claims Office were simple and based largely on the many successful attempts he had made while playing the 'Game of Your Life' in virtual reality on his computer screen.

He planned to walk up to the Claims Office entrance

# THE GAME OF YOUR LIFE

line carrying a protest sign and wearing a scarf over his mouth, as if the blend in with the various protesters that were usually there. When he was close enough to the entrance door, which stands adjacent to the exit door he would slip in the exit door, drawing the security guards attention while he handcuffed the entrance and exit doors together. Once the security guard stopped what he was doing and walked over to check his I.D. Randy planned to put his protest poster down reach in his backpack for his I.D. but pull out his stun gun and stun him.

After that he would take the freight elevator, not the visitors elevator, up to the penthouse floor where the claims office was. Once on the penthouse floor he deliberately pause for a moment while the chaos for the commotion from people on line downstairs locked out by the handcuffed entrance and exit doors engulfs security and most likely mesmerizes the Claims office receptionist watching her computer security screen. Then he would take his seltzer capsule, put it in his mouth and let it fume up and spoil out of his mouth. At that point he would run out into the reception area, all doubled over, moaning and spitting, slobbering and stumbling while trying to get the receptionist attention. Once she leaves her desk to see what is wrong he would point to his stomach and say emergency. At that point

# THE GAME OF YOUR LIFE

she should have figured out that he needed medical attention and would go back to her desk to call security and an ambulance. As soon as she turns to go back to her desk to make the calls, Randy would follow her back and grab her electronic key card and run to the Claims Clerks Office; use her key to gain entry and accomplish his mission. The standing rule is, once he was inside the Claims Clerks Office he was entitled to get paid.

Randy commands 40G to pause the file feed and to delete all references to his plan and route. He got up from the table with the intent of going upstairs, taking his shower, and getting dressed. Then going into his office and get the printout of his maps, then go online and validate his claim voucher.

Once all of those steps had been completed Randy would go out to his garage and get in his car and the adventure would begin; but there was one fatal flaw in his plan. Unless each element of his plan was followed precisely disaster would loom. That was exactly what happened. Randy made one small but critical mistake in his planned routine; he didn't follow his plan to the letter.

Randy got up from the table went upstairs, went online

# THE GAME OF YOUR LIFE

and validated his Claim Voucher for the full $70,000.00 for the 32 day period, then went to take his shower and all hell broke loose.

Immediately following Randy's inputting his Claim Voucher request he noticed that the total missed valid, claims for this date was $10 million dollars and his pin number was 012345678910111-2, which was very easy to commit to memory. Randy printed out the Claim voucher receipt out and laid it on top of his clothes before he walked into the bathroom to shower. This move as was expected flagged him as a Game of your Life player before he was ready to play.

# THE GAME OF YOUR LIFE

## CHAPTER 2

# THE PLAN OF ATTACK

Just 24 hours earlier

Lou Walker an avid part time video game quality assurance agent was seated on a bar stool at his neighborhood pub monitoring the lives of three different citizens as one of his subscriber reality shows.

Lou had been tossing back tequila with a beer back since he got off of work at the UPS station down the street. Lou was a regular and has a standing 'catch a cab home account' attached to his bar tab just in case.

Lou has been employed as a delivery driver for UPS for almost 22 years working various commercial and residential routes during that time. Lately Lou had increased his focus and commitment to monitoring at least three random people a month to see if he could catch or hi-jack a Claimer.

# THE GAME OF YOUR LIFE

Because of his hours he rarely has a chance to stake out the Video Game Players Claims Office during their peak hours. The time of day when most, if not all, of the gamers arrive to submit their 32 day cycle claims vouchers.

Since Lou was a former college Football player he knows he has the skills to chase down and subdue the average Video Game Player, looking to submit a big claim.

Lou took the whole week off to make that dream come true. Lou always believed that his drinking habits and his work habits were separate and distinct activities. But lately his health has been deteriorating more and more rapidly while his medical cost were starting to mound up. Lou had started to take more and more time off from work to go to rehab and he wasn't going to alert his healthcare provider for risk of losing his job. So he covered the cost right out of his own pocket and that was really beginning to take a toll on him.

Lou also believed if he could take down one video game player, looking to submit an average size voucher say for at least $10 thousand dollars, he would have enough money to take his wife and kids on the vacation of a life time. Between the $5 thousand dollar reward

# THE GAME OF YOUR LIFE

and his 32 day claim, Lou would have well over $10 thousand dollars in his pocket.

The three gamers Lou has spent the last 32 days watching, while he kept up his regular game playing included Randy Hatchfield. Lou had seen Randy on prior occasions at the Claims Office and knew he was the kind of guy who would someday muster up the courage to submit the big claim and be placed into play as a participant of the 'Game of Your Life.' From all indications, after watching Randy's daily activities live and through his teabow account, Lou was positive Randy was ready to make the big claim.

Lou's game plan was slightly different from most of the other video game players who have turned Big Claim Hi-Jackers. Lou's plan wasn't limited to waiting downstairs at the Claims office and either bum rushing the prospects and robbing them right there of their claim voucher or just getting close enough to them in the crowd and picking their pocket. Lou planned to use his work uniform as a rouse and just walk up to Randy's house, ring the door bell and jump him right there in the doorway, and take the claim voucher right then.

# THE GAME OF YOUR LIFE

With this strategy Lou could avoid the tag along strategy many other claim hi-jackers used. The tag along strategy was simple enough: the prospective claims hi-jacker would join forces with another; one would monitor the whereabouts of the prospective victim and keep in constant communications with the other hi-jacker via iphone or texting. When the victim reached a vulnerable location, while in route to submit their claim, the monitoring hi-jacker would jump him. The value of the tow men monitoring was based on a key glitch in the video tracking system. Eventhough one or both of the hijackers had a Premium Television Subscriber package, when a PNC number moved from one video providers service area to another roaming charges were applied. And that process required handing off the live video feed from one provider to the other and could take upwards of 3 minutes to be accomplished.

During that 3 minute blackout if you didn't have your eyes physically on the PNC you could lose them. The robbery of the Claim voucher receipt usually takes place relatively swiftly since the monitor knows exactly where the victim has hidden his voucher receipt. Most of the time a simple push and grab occurred. The national surveillance system kind of takes the mystery out of not only tracking the victim but also tracking the

# THE GAME OF YOUR LIFE

perpetrator as well. It kind of levels the playing field and the penalty for this crime is usually severe. But that just makes this game so much more intriguing.

To further explain the roaming signal glitch: The FCC has implemented a cross subscriber monitoring rule. With so many people monitoring other peoples activities the FCC came up with the cross subscriber access monitoring rule. Which means that the signal one cable company offers its subscribers is required to be interrupted for at least 3 minutes when the subscriber video feed crosses into another provider's field of service, or roams into another provider's service area. Simply put it works just like the wireless telephone service provider's system; if you want to be connected to video feed in another video provider's service area your provider must accept the roaming charges and then you are reconnected. Each provider bill's your account at the end of the billing cycle. This also discourages career claim voucher bandit's efforts to follow prospects on day's other than the 33$^{rd}$ day of a Claim period.

Lou has had limited success in hi-jacking Claims vouchers over the years but he was confident that he could pull this one off. He figured he would arrive in uniform, hand Randy an empty cardboard box with a

# THE GAME OF YOUR LIFE

few international stickers on it, and his signature clipboard. Then as Randy attempts to determine who the box is from, Lou planned to taze him, tie him up and go look for his claims voucher receipt.

As for the second half of Lou's plan, his journey to riches, the claiming of both his and Randy's vouchers; Lou planned to wait until 11:00pm the final hour of the claim day, and then go to the claims office in hopes that the crowd of voucher pirates would have thinned out to only the hardcore few. Then just bully his way in before the clock strikes 12:00 midnight.
12 hours earlier

Seated in front of his 175 square inch hi-definition 3D Panasonic wall unit was Miles Moore. Moore had been a mail carrier assigned to the Oval Dr, Lane, and Avenue route for the last 18 months.

Miles was a 24 year old scrapping young blue eyed blonde recently married with twins and a very unhappy wife since loosing her girlish figure with the birth of their two darling young boys Jeff and Jeb.

Lately Miles had become more and more obsessed with winning some extra money through hi-jacking video gamers entered in the 'Game of Your Life' reality

34

# THE GAME OF YOUR LIFE

show, because he had fallen behind in his weekly payments to his bookie. You see Miles had a little, as he called it, gambling problem; which had caused him to fear losing his job at the post office. Miles had been told on several occasions that he could not receive visitors on the job unless they were immediate family, such as his wife or child. This had given him more incentive to not fall behind on his weekly tab and not only run the risk of a couple of broken ribs but the risk of losing his job as well.

Miles had spent countless hours watching random game players attempt to settle their voucher claims, plotting and planning how to I.D. the big claimers before they were overwhelmed by the more seasoned hi-jackers.

Day after day Miles spent three to four hours studying the movements of prospective big claimers, to the point he now believed he could almost smell a big claim voucher holder. And he is hot on the trail of Randy Hatchfield today. Miles, a North East Communications Premium Package subscriber, the same pay for television provider used by many of the residents on his mail route, had devised a fool proof plan on how to hi-jack prospective big voucher claimers.

# THE GAME OF YOUR LIFE

His plan was to merely walk up on any prospective big claim receipt holder, who lived on his route, while he was in uniform and carrying their mail. Hand them a fake registered letter from the Video Game company demanding that they mail in their voucher receipt instead of bringing it to the office in person. The letter would come in an official looking certified mail envelope with a return post paid envelope inside of it. Miles believed that the claimant would only ask if the post office could get it there the same day. Of course he would swear to it and off he'd go.

Part two of this master plan which called for Miles to collect on the now pilfered ticket, was a no brainer, all he had to do was walk up to the main door of the Video Game company's Claim Office with the certified envelope in hand looking for the Claims Clerks signature and he would be paid.

Once the company has the claim voucher receipt in hand they are obligated to pay it in the form preferred by the presenter which could be in the form of a prepaid cash card. If an agent presents it then the card is provided but the PIN number is mailed to the claimant via certified mail.

# THE GAME OF YOUR LIFE

Midnight the 33$^{rd}$ Day Global Video Game Developers Claims Office

Vice President Thom Gullota and Corporate Intern Bill Mahner have just arrived to prepare for the days activities.

Bill was standing at the Claims Office door waiting for authorization to enter when Thom stepped off of the elevator and said, Hello. Bill smiled and cheerfully responded, "Good morning, I mean good evening Mr. Gullota, how are you this evening?" Thom smiled and said, "Why I'm just fine, Bill isn't it?" Bill said, yes Mr. Gullota I am Bill Mahner the new intern from corporate. I recognize you from all of the photo's of you and the chairman hanging in the corporate office lobby in Chicago. Photo's of all of the awards that you and your team have won over the years. I have always wanted to meet you."
As the two men walked by the receptionist desk in the lobby Thom pulled out his magnetic key card and used it to open the office door, then he extended his hand to welcome Bill inside.

Then the two men shuck hands and entered the office. That was when Thom told Bill to have a seat in the

# THE GAME OF YOUR LIFE

office waiting area while he went to settle into his office and reset the security alarm.

Bill sat in awe, stirring at the wall of monitors that control the corporate subscriber list and client database, of all of the company's 30 million video game quality assurance agents. Then he saw the Claims Office award wall for excellence in Customer and Agent Service. There must have been a hundred of them each coming at the end of calendar quarter since the company started some 25 years ago.

The next thing that caught Bills eye was the glass enclosed armory. He thought he had seen large weapons arsenals on television and in clips in video games but none was more impressive or as large and seemingly complete as this one. From handguns to automatic rifles, bulletproof vest, helmets, lazar rifles and stun guns it was like looking into the national museum of fire arms only without the tanks and such.

After a few moments Thom returned and invited Bill to come into his office to chat before he assigned him his duties.

When Bill entered Thom's 800 square foot corner penthouse office he was again amazed not only at the

# THE GAME OF YOUR LIFE

views of the city but the lavishness of the office. Thom had every comfort imaginable from a 50' x 50' indoor lap pool to a full spa with sauna and steam room, exercise equipment and a modern chef's kitchen. Bill was afraid to ask if Thom had a bedroom in it so he just smiled and said, "This is the nicest office I've ever seen" and sat down in front of Thom's massive glass desk.

While Bill sat and listened, Thom went over his daily, weekly and monthly routine. Then he gave Bill his standard new intern speech about corporate commitment, the theory of dog eat dog, his philosophy on profits first, and his strategy for dealing with the competition. Simply put, 'slash and burn them all as quickly as possible.'

Then Thom summed up Bill's duties, strongly suggesting that he focus on assisting him only. Primarily shadowing him and learning the business from the executive prospective as thoroughly as possible over the next 12 months. Then he went over his personal calendar so that the two would be in sync.

Thom pointed out that while Bill was single, he had two children and a career wife; who happened to be the

# THE GAME OF YOUR LIFE

Police Commissioner. One of the reasons Thom's operation was so successful and cost efficient.

Thom explained that he would be leaving on a two week vacation later on that morning and expected Bill to brush up on all of the corporate operating policies while he was gone, even though Thom would be in constant touch with his Assistant Vice President. Bill was excited but reserved and very agreeable.

Then the conversation turned to compensation. Thom explained that as an intern Bill knew he wasn't entitled to compensation, his college credits were more than enough to compensate him for his time and commitment. But Thom knew he had, had great success in training and developing junior executives when they were compensated in some way or form.

Thom tried to make his compensation policy as simple as possible. He told Bill if he worked hard, stayed away from voucher hi-jacking activities in any form, he would submit his name for a monthly scholarship award, every month that he continues his internship. The money could be used for any purpose and if he left school he did not have to repay it. Thom told Bill that the money comes out of the offices monthly bonus program and without explaining how it worked in detail

# THE GAME OF YOUR LIFE

he said, for every voucher claim that we avoid having to pay we get ten percent. The amount allocated for scholarships has averaged $10,000 a month. Bill's eyes almost popped out of his head when he heard that and his loyalty commitment meter went from 99% to 1,000% in less than one second flat.

Then Thom said, "The monthly bonus is paid on the 15th of each month and this months projection is on target. Now for the downside of the business, you noticed the awards wall outside? That is the result of never, not making bonus. This company has one simple rule, if you miss bonus we'll miss you. That means if you miss your bonus goal for the month you won't be around for the next bonus period and that includes everyone in your office. I have a staff of 50 people including technicians, bookkeepers and executive assistants and now you, don't let me down."

Bill enthusiastically responded and said, "You can count on me." Thom replied, "Great I knew I could, but keep in mind there are camera's everywhere and we have a duty of fair play with our Gaming Agents. We can do no harm if they make it to the office and present a valid voucher receipt, we must honor it. We can't hide from it. We can not, not take it and then make believe

# THE GAME OF YOUR LIFE

we didn't receive it. But all else is fair game. Enough said, are your ready to begin your new career?"

Bill said, "I am but I do have one question." Thom responded and said, "Great, fire away." Bill sat back and said, "Just how does the company make money to pay such heavy bonuses?"

Thom said, "Great question. In a nutshell, we make money on death. Either by presenting video games that depicts deadly activities, or on the video's we make of those game agents attempting to hi-jack other agents vouchers and most especially on the actual deaths of either the voucher hi-jackers or their victims."

Bill smiled and said, "So you're talking about the applicant insurance policies?"
Thom said, "Bing! We are the only communications service providers who provide that benefit to all of our gaming agents. It allows for their families to benefit and for us to position ourselves to replace or recover from the lost of good qualified game testing agents. The 50/50 sharing of the life insurance benefit payout continues to keep us in bonus and the game testers families from complaining. Their accidental or violent deaths also keep us in video footage with a mountain of game development ideas in the wings."

# THE GAME OF YOUR LIFE

## CHAPTER 3

# SO WHO WANTS TO PLAY?

Randy Hatchfield's Front Door

As soon as Randy began his shower he looked through the upstairs bathroom window and noticed a UPS truck was just pulling up to his walkway. So even though he was now soaking wet he attempted to be proactive and grabbed his bath towel, stepped into his shower shoes and ran downstairs to answer the door.

With water dripping from his head to his feet Randy left a trail of wet footprints and little pools of water from the upstairs bathroom to the downstairs front door.

Positioning himself behind the door, Randy stood at the ready to open the door, receive whatever package and take the signature apparatus the driver presented.

Unfortunately the best plans of mice and men is not just a clique. When Lou rang the door bell Randy opened

# THE GAME OF YOUR LIFE

the front door and reached for the package. As he did, his towel slide to the floor and he bent over to grab it. Using everything he had Lou put his shoulder to the middle of the door and pushed it open knocking Randy back against the foyer wall in the buff. Lou stepped inside and looked over Randy laying on the floor and assumed he had knocked him into the livingroom. When he turned to look he placed his foot right in one of Randy's footprints and his steel toed sneaker lost traction and he fell backwards and hit his head against the door jam and knocked himself out cold.

Randy scrambled back to his feet and grabbed his towel. Then he looked at Lou and assumed this was all a freak accident. On his way to the kitchen to get his first aide kit he accidently kicked the package Lou had was attempting to deliver and realized it was just an empty box. That was the moment when it hit him, Lou was not delivering a package he was attempting to hijack his Claim Voucher Receipt. Randy quickly realized that by him logging in his claim before he was ready to leave had made him vulnerable to any and all hi-jackers as his name and intentions were now uploaded and he was right in the middle of the 'Game of Your Life' for real, for real.

# THE GAME OF YOUR LIFE

Now perplexed, not knowing what might happen next, Randy reached in the kitchen pantry for a roll of duck tape. Wrapped a length around his towel and his waist and then ran back over to the UPS guy and tied his hands behind his back and his feet together.

Lou began to stir so Randy duck taped his eyes and his mouth being careful to leave his nose unobstructed. Then Randy dragged Lou into the kitchen and pushed him down the basement stairwell.

Now visibly shaken, Randy went back to close the front door and realized that the truck Lou came in was still parked out front with the engine running. Randy immediately ran upstairs and got dressed. Then he ran back downstairs, went outside, and pulled the UPS truck around and parked it on the other side of the street and then turned it off and walked back inside of the house.

That was just enough time for Randy to realize the opportunity he had. He hurried back in and went downstairs to search Lou for his voucher receipt. Just as Lou was regaining conscientious Randy pulled Lou's claim voucher receipt out of his back pocket and glanced at it. With Lou now wiggling around, Randy was forced to cold cock him and reinforce his ties.

# THE GAME OF YOUR LIFE

Just as Randy began to walk back up stairs the door bell rang again. When he got to the top of the stairwell he shouted, "Who is it?" And the voice replied "Mail man." Randy yelled back, "Ok! Just leave it in the box, will ya?" The mailman responded, "Certified letter, I need a signature or I'll have to return it to the post office for delivery tomorrow."

Now somewhat skeptical Randy yelled back, "Ok do that!" Miles responded and said, "Are you sure Mr. Hatchfield this might be very important?" Randy said, "Oh! Is that you Miles?" Miles said, "Yea and can you hurried up, I'm already way behind."

Randy said, "Give me a second, I'll be right there." As Randy stepped back into the kitchen from the basement stairwell he thought to grab his baseball bat just in case and when he approached the front door this time he laid the baseball bat in the door path wedging it between the foyer wall and the bottom of the door. Then he narrowly opened the door.

Miles handed him the clipboard sideways which allowed Randy to relax when he grabbed it. Then he handed Randy the certified envelope and then, when he went to hand Randy a pen to write with it he

# THE GAME OF YOUR LIFE

deliberately dropped to the floor. Again, Randy bent down to pick it up and Miles leaped up into the air and drop kicked the door so hard it came off of its hinges and fell on him. Miles stepped inside and stood on top of the door for a moment as it rested on Randy's back.

Then Miles stepped further inside, off of the now broken door which was resting on Randy's back and turned to bend and lift the door off of the now dazed Randy.

Miles began to rifle through Randy's pants pockets and shirt pocket kicking him two or three times in the side after he looked in each pocket.

Randy was now disoriented, couching up blood and semi conscientious. The longer it took Miles to go through each of Randy's pockets the more violent, angry and aggressive he became. Finally when he finished looking in Randy's left side pockets and was about to kick him some more Randy had reached back and grabbed the baseball bat he had wedged in between the front door and foyer wall and with one major league swing, he hit Miles in the shin and you could hear it his left leg break in half. Miles came crashing down like a ton of bricks right beside Randy, grabbing for his shin and screaming at the top of his lungs.

# THE GAME OF YOUR LIFE

That's was when Randy pulled himself together and stood up over Miles. Miles attempted to wave Randy off because he was now incapacitated and in excruciating pain. But Randy saw this as his opportunity for revenge and wailed all over Miles' with no less than 10 blows.

When Randy finally came to his senses he and realized what he was doing he stopped in mid swing and looked down at Miles' broken and bloody body. Miles was limp but still moaning and begging him to stop.

Randy looked around at all of the blood on the floor, walls and ceiling, his clothes, hands and the bat, which was still in his hand. He throw up right there all over Miles' body. Miles had now stopped moaning and his eyes had rolled back in his head.

Randy let the bat slip out of his hand and started to hyper ventilate. He stumbled back into the kitchen and sat down at the table. Then he got up and returned to Miles' body, rifled through his pockets to retrieve his Claim voucher receipt which was worth $5,000.00 and thought about his death benefit share.

# THE GAME OF YOUR LIFE

Now parked down the street was the ACME LAWN CARE truck which had pulled up and stopped when Randy moved the UPS truck earlier.

Now facing the biggest dilemma of his life; whether to continue on with his plan for financial freedom or wait and explain to the police what just happened, Randy quickly figured out how to have his cake and eat it too.

Randy went upstairs and got his backpack, then came back downstairs and went into the kitchen and looked in the tool closet and got a hammer and some nails. He immediately nailed the front door up then turned and pulled Miles' body towards the kitchen so he could push it down into the basement next to Lou.

Just as he turned the corner into the kitchen he realized that the lawn guys had finished the neighbors yard and were about to begin trimming and cutting the lawn in his backyard. This was a major problem because the basement door faced his glass patio doors. Randy ran to the patio door and tried to wave the lawn guys to go away. He yelled through the doorway that he didn't want service this week, because it was going to rain. Since the men did not understand english very well, Randy had to leave Miles' body in the foyer and go outside onto the patio to explain.

# THE GAME OF YOUR LIFE

Randy walked outside just as almost all of the landscape crew had finished up and were walking back around to the front of the house to begin work there. The only one left in the patio area was Miguel. Miguel was from El Salvador and understood English very well. Although Miguel was older, about 60 years of age he looked as if he was 45. He was a very quiet hard working guy who stood about 5'2" tall with a slight build and well respected by the other workers.

Randy walked over to Miguel and said, "Miguel how are you today?" Miguel responded and said, "Senor Hatchfield I am fine, how are you?" Randy now a little flustered said, "Look it is about to rain, can you guy's come back later in the week?" Miguel smiled and said, "Si, no senor Hatchfield. This is the assigned day to do your yard. If we miss today we will not be paid and Mr. Greenberg will be very mad. But if you like I can call him and tell him what you would like?" Randy looked around for a moment and then he said, "Well I really have to leave, I am running late." Miguel said, "Si, usually you are long gone when we arrive. Is everything alright Senor Hatchfield?"

# THE GAME OF YOUR LIFE

Randy started to respond and then he just stared at Miguel for a moment and shook his head; no, then started to back away.

Miguel reached in his back pocket and pulled out a 5 inch paring knife and started to clean his fingernails with it as he spoke. He said, "Senor Hatchfield, I see you are a famous man. Your name, your face, your house is all over the television set. You are playing the 'Game of Your Life', huh?" Randy just froze and stared.

Miguel repeated his statement this time using the paring knife to emphasize every word by pointing it in Randy's face. Randy backed up some more and slowly reached with his left hand down at his cargo pants pocket. Miguel smiled and said, "No, no, no Senor Hatchfield. I don't think you are fast enough to reach into your pant pocket and get your knife before I can use mine." And he jabbed at Randy three short jabs with the knife. Each time Randy jumped back and to the right away from the doorway.

Miguel became more and more aggressive jabbing harder and closer to Randy's face each time. All the while Randy was reaching closer and closer at that left pants pocket. Just as Randy got closed enough to the

# THE GAME OF YOUR LIFE

pocket to feel the closed flap Miguel lunged at him cutting his left shirt sleeve and saying "No, no, no Senor Hatchfield.

That's when Randy's right hand pulled out his taser and shot Miguel in the abdomen. The taser was turned up to 100,000 volts and as Miguel shook and trembled violently out of control Randy reached over to the porch screen door and grabbed a hand hoe and crowned Miguel in the top of his head.
With blood splattered everywhere Miguel fell to the ground. Randy quickly rifled through Miguel's pockets and found is Claim Voucher receipt which meant $5,000.00 to the barer plus a share of his insurance money.

Now Randy knew he had a real problem he started back into the house to clean up and change his clothes, when one of Miguel's co-workers returned to hurry him up and saw him laying on the back patio bleeding from the head and neck. Then he ran back to their truck to screaming for his co-workers to call an ambulance.

Randy rushed up stairs changed and quickly washed up. On his way back downstairs he saw a police car pull up to the back of the lawn crew's truck and people starting to point at his house. Randy knew right then if he was

# THE GAME OF YOUR LIFE

to succeed he would have to slip by those cops and get to the Claims Clerk's office. Fortunately for him in those days and times, murder for profit carried a trouble price and without the game claim money, he could never afford to pay his way out of jail.

So Randy ran down the stairs and slipped out the patio door on his way to the garage. Randy had a one and a half car garage set back on the far end of his property, literally at the far end of his backyard. It was so far back its entrance sat on the next street over. Randy's front door was on Oval Drive while his garage entrance was on Oval Drive Lane. Both streets lay on adjacent cul-de-sacs that let out on Lake Drive.

Randy slipped into the back door of the garage and instead of taking his car into town he decided to take his classic 10 speed bike. It would give him greater maneuverability in either a car or foot chase he figured. He decided to roll the bike out of the garages side door instead of risking alerting the police who were now on his patio, where he was.

Standing outside the garage side door was Linda Leah, a 14 year old blonde hair, blue eyed, neighborhood loud mouth who hated him with a passion. She never quit forgave him for running over her cat last winter. Even

# THE GAME OF YOUR LIFE

though she called the police and they told her they could do nothing about it, because it actually seemed like it was an accident.

When Randy stepped out of the garage side door and saw her standing there he knew she was up to something but he had hoped that she wouldn't give him away if he was nice to her. But Linda was the kind of person whom nothing or no one could satisfy, no matter how much they tried.

Randy stepped out and rolled his bike out behind him. Linda said, "Good morning Mr. Hatchfield" in her most sarcastic voice. "Where are you going so early? She continued."

Randy thought he'd better placate her so he could get on his way as quickly as possible. So he responded, "Why? Linda! You never showed any interest in my daily routine before! Why now?" Linda smiled and said, "Right, I actually hate your guts you murderer. But I saw what you did to that Spanish man, on TV and now your trying to get away right? But first you have to redeem his Claims receipts, right? I want them. I want them in exchange for you killing my cat Percy, last year. You know the little cat you murdered last winter. So give them to me."

# THE GAME OF YOUR LIFE

Randy thought for a second and then said, "No way! Now move out of my way." Linda said, "I said give them to me, right now or I'll scream and the police will get you. So you better comply."

Randy smiled and said, "You saw what I am capable of, little girl, so if I were you, I'd get out of my way before something bad happens to you too."

Linda said, "You can't do anything to me, you cat and Mexican murderer and who knows who else you've murdered today. Look the police are going into your house, any other dead bodies in there? Mr. Murderer?"

Randy reached over at Linda and she recoiled and took a deep breathe and said, "I mean it, give me those Claim vouchers, right now, or I'll scream."

Randy pushed pass her and attempted to mount his bike to ride off. Linda grabbed hold of his backpack and started to scream as he tried to pull away. Randy stood up and began to peddle hard and she continued to hold on. Randy could see the police officers starting to look in his direction. So he peddled even harder. Linda continued to hold on and slow him down while she screamed. Randy swatted back at her but could not

# THE GAME OF YOUR LIFE

reach her and she started to dig her heels in and drag her feet making it harder and harder for him to pull away. Just as the police men reached the front of his garage and stepped into the street, Randy pulled in between two large oak trees knocking Linda's arm away and throwing her to the ground.

As he quickly pulled away he looked back at her, sliding and rolling under a parked car, he began weaving in and out of the tree line. One officer stopped to aid Linda as Randy pulled around the corner. The other officer stopped running behind Randy and pulled out his touch phone to call for help.

Randy figured the two officers would be tied up at his house for a couple of hours untying Lou, processing Miles and Miguel and tending to Linda, so as he rode past his house to get out of the cul-da-sac and saw their police cars door still open and running he decided to steal it. Right then Randy got off of his bike and put it in the back of the patrol car then drove off.

# THE GAME OF YOUR LIFE

## CHAPTER 4

# IN HOT PURSUIT

The Crime Scene

Officers Frank Ore and Jake Thomas were trying to comfort little Linda Leah after Randy rode off on his bicycle knocking her to the ground. Ofc. Ore asked Linda if she was alright and she said, she didn't know if she could walk and she started to cry. Ofc. Thomas then said, "Frank why don't you go back to the crime scene and call this in. She doesn't look like she is going to need to go to the hospital and I can finish taking her statement here and meet you back there." Linda interrupted and said, "Am I going to have to go to the hospital?" Ofc. Thomas said, "Sadly young lady I don't think so. Do you want us to call your mother?" And Linda said, "She is at work. I think I can make it home now." Ofc. Thomas said, "Before you go, tell me exactly what happened."

Linda slowly stood up and said, "I was just standing by the tree there and he came out the garage over there and flew right by me. I tried to wave good morning and I thing my hand got caught in his backpack strap and the next thing I knew I was under this car."

# THE GAME OF YOUR LIFE

Ofc. Thomas then said, "Did he say anything to you?"

Linda thought for a moment and said, "No he is usually very rude like that, but you get used to it. Can I go home now? My back is hurting. And my neck too."

Ofc. Thomas looked at her, smiled and then said, "Here is my card when your parents get home you can have them call me if you need to go to the hospital or anything, ok?" Linda slowly walked away and said, "Thank you Officer Thomas. You are so kind."

By the time Ofc. Thomas returned to the patio area, Ofc. Ore had looked through the house and found both Miles and Lou in the basement. He was in the process of calling for another ambulance when Ofc. Thomas stepped in and asked what was going on.

Ofc. Ore turned and said, "I have called for a another bus and the detectives squad. You know we had an assault victim on the patio that was badly injured and unconscious; when I got back I heard some screaming coming from the basement and went down to investigate. I found that UPS driver tied up with duck tape seemingly assaulted as well and the body of this mailman seemingly beaten to death with a blunt object

# THE GAME OF YOUR LIFE

maybe that bat over there. The victim doesn't seem to have been dead too long and was about to take a statement from the UPS guy. Preliminarily it seems each of them was assaulted for no reason. My guess is the homeowner just snapped."

Then he walked back upstairs and started to examine the nailed up front door. Ofc. Thomas followed him up and said, "Frank! You believe the owner snapped? Is that your assessment of what happened here? Really?" Ofc. Ore looked back at Ofc. Thomas and said, "That is what is going in my report, why? You got a problem with that assessment? Tell it to the Desk Sergeant." Ofc. Thomas stood back and then said, "I'm not going to tell the Desk Sergeant any thing. But if you want me to tell the Desk Sgt. anything I can tell him that you have been inordinately obsessed with that palm pilot of yours watching that reality show. And the truth be told I believe this guy here is the one you have been watching. Now I can tell the Desk Sgt. that, if you'd like."

Ofc. Ore stared back at Ofc. Thomas and finally said, "They told me to watch out for you. They told me you were a snitch. I thought they were all wrong but now I see they were right. You tell the Desk Sgt. What you

# THE GAME OF YOUR LIFE

want. I'm a good cop and my record speaks for itself. You little rat."

Then Ofc. Ore kicked the front door open and started to walk towards there patrol car, which was no longer there. He walked right up to where he had parked it not realizing that he was walking up to an empty space. When he got there the second ambulance pulled up and parked right in the empty space.

That was when Ofc. Ore turned to Ofc. Thomas and said, "So where is the stupid car?" Ofc. Thomas said, "I don't know, it was right there when we left it."
Then Ofc. Ore stomped his foot and almost blew a gasket saying, "I'll bet that fool on the bike came around here and took that damn car to the Claims Clerks Office."

Ofc. Thomas said, "You buggin man, you been playing that damn game to long. Everything you see is about that stupid game. Just call the Desk Sgt. and ask him to put out an A.P.B. for a stolen patrol car."

Ofc. Ore pulled out his touch phone and opened up his video communications app and tuned into Randy Hatchfields PNC number and got a roaming notice but he immediately saw his patrol car stopped at the

# THE GAME OF YOUR LIFE

intersection of Walsingham Road and Lake Dr. He turned to Ofc. Thomas and said, "That little bastard is on his way to the Claims Clerks office I know it. We need a car, right now. I estimate by the time this feed reconnects he will be either on I-688 or making his way over to Vonn Road."

Then Ofc. Thomas said, "Why don't you just call the Desk Sgt. and report the car stolen!" Ofc. Ore snapped back and said, "Look rookie, I'm the lead officer in this patrol and we'll handle this my way. I'm not going to embarrass myself and our unit by calling the Desk Sgt. and reporting that my patrol car was stolen. Do I make myself clear? And don't bring it up again. Now go into the house and see if our perp left his car keys hanging somewhere." Ofc. Thomas then said, "But the procedure is to call it in." Ofc. Ore snapped back in a loud voice and said, "Did you here that order rookie or is this job to difficult for you?" Ofc. Thomas said, "Not a problem but this is going into my daily report."

Ofc. Ore said, "Screw your daily report now get a move on it."

By the time Ofc. Thomas returned with the car keys Randy had left on a wall hook in the kitchen, Ofc. Ore was briefing the detectives assigned to the murder of the mailman. Ofc. Thomas walked up on the men talking and before he could say a word, Ofc. Ore turned and told him to go get the car and bring it around immediately. Ofc. Thomas went and brought the car around.

When Ofc. Thomas returned with Randy's car, Ofc. Ore was standing in front of the house impatiently waiting. Ofc. Thomas pulled up and Ofc. Ore jumped in and said, "Ok! Lets get out of here. It looks like this Hatchfield guy running up Walsingham towards Vonn Road right about now. ...I'm not sure if we are going to catch him before he gets there. But if he does make it there, we are going to be in a quandary. You see he'll be in a roaming zone again and we'll lose his signal for 3 more minutes. The problem is he will have the advantage of continuing on, on Walsingham to I-688 or going north up Vonn. If he takes Walsingham he'll have a straight shot to the Claims Clerks office a total distance of 7 miles. But if he's smart, he will continue up Vonn Road and then make his way over to the Claims Clerks office. ...The benefit in taking Vonn Road is we might never know when he gets off to go across town towards the Claims Office. He could literally weave in and out of the roaming zone locking out video signal for 3 minute blocks of time at a clip each time he does it. And with 3 minutes of unseen

# THE GAME OF YOUR LIFE

driving time, once inside the business district, he could be anywhere when video reconnects." Ofc. Thomas then said, "Why don't we just go to the Claims Office directly and just wait for him there?"

Ofc. Ore said, "A typical rookie question. … If we can't stop him before he gets close enough to the claims office we probably won't stop him at all. He already has the opportunity of dumping the patrol car at any time while he is in the roaming zone and once he presents his claim receipt he maybe rich enough to buy off his prosecution fines." Ofc. Thomas then said, "Is that what you are worried about? Or are you more interested in catching him so you could get a hold of his claim voucher receipt for yourself?" Ofc. Ore looked at him and then said, "You keep your eyes open for that patrol car, I'll worry about prosecuting this perpetrator."

Inside the stolen Patrol Car

As soon as Randy got into the patrol car he noticed that the lights were still flashing in the rear window, so he scanned the on board computer console and found the on off switch turned the lights off and took off.

# THE GAME OF YOUR LIFE

As he drove through the neighborhood he could hear
the police car dispatcher calling out various numeric
codes and seemingly sending patrol units all over the
city. This was exciting at first but Randy was now way
out of his league and definitely off his planned course
for the day. The one positive thing at that moment was,
the fact that the patrol car was an upgraded, unmarked
black Crown Victoria. And that meant the engine had
been replaced with an light weight aluminum one, all of
the glass was bullet proof and the tires were practically
indestructible.

Randy knew he wasn't going to get to the Claims
Clerks office in a City patrol car so he thought through
the best route to take to avoid the police who were now
certainly mad as heck and looking for their patrol car at
every turn.

Randy recalculated his planned route to the Claims
Clerks office. The distance from his house on Oval
Drive to Global Video Game Development Claims
Office was approximately 10 miles. The quickest route
was to take the 2 block drive from Oval Drive to Lake
Drive, and then make a right turn onto Walsingham
Road, I-688 East. Next take I-688 North approximately
6 1/4 miles veer left onto Ulmerton Road for 3 miles.
Make a left onto 130th Ave. North for 6 blocks then

# THE GAME OF YOUR LIFE

make a right onto 125th St. for another 3 blocks, make a right onto 134th Ave. North; and travel the final 2 blocks to the corporate driveway and enter on the left.

Critical to the success of Randy's route would be his ability to negotiate the route and take advantage of the six Television and Communications Networks service areas he would travel through to get to the Claims Clerks Office at 3500 134th Ave., Ridgecrest Park, Pinellas County.

Since each network had its own subscriber network and equal access to all video and security feeds in their service area. Randy's plan hinged on the fact that all networks signal areas overlapped with others. And some networks do not have all access to all video system feeds. But more importantly all network systems faced the same roaming signal black out glitch. Which usually last up to 3 minutes, but that wasn't guaranteed since some providers roaming signals either only faded out for less than 45 second before it reconnected its subscribers.

With that piece of information now clearly ringing in his head, Randy decided to use an alternative route which laid out this way: He would drive the Police Car up Oval Drive to Lake Drive pass over Walsingham

# THE GAME OF YOUR LIFE

Road I-688 North into the gated community of Big Oak Valley which was just across Hibiscus Road... Then get on Vonn Road and go north. Vonn Road was the border between both the North East Communications Network and Mid City Communications Networks service areas. Then he would go east along 134th Ave over to 121st St. dump the patrol car and use his inline roller skates to make the final ½ mile trip along 121st St. to 3500 134th Ave. the entrance to Global Video Game Development Claims Office complex. Then he would slip upstairs to the penthouse office on the 33rd floor and present his Claim vouchers and receipts.

Trying to stay under the speed limit and watching other drivers slow down as he approached them, Randy continued to check out the interior of the unmarked patrol car. But there was plenty of chatter on the car radio and as Randy drove up one block and down another in hopes of using the tree lined streets to obscure his presence from any surveillance cameras, he noticed the numbers 456 prominently displayed on the dashboard and the onboard computer counsel.

At first Randy didn't pay much attention to the numbers as displayed but after a few minutes of travel he kept hearing the radio dispatcher call for 'Unit 456'. After the forth time the dispatcher said, "Patrol 456 10-4?"

# THE GAME OF YOUR LIFE

That was when Randy realized that the dispatcher was talking to him. After pushing several keys and turning some dials on the on board computer console Randy heard the dispatcher say, "Patrol 456 10-4 final request." That was when Randy panicked and shouted, "10-4, 10-4 dispatch." The dispatcher paused for a moment and responded, "Frank?" And Randy said, "Frank is taking a leek." Then the dispatcher said, "Jake? Is that you?" Randy responded and said, "Yes Sir." Then dispatcher paused and said, "Look Rookie we have very specific protocols for using the radio. Get with it and have your superior contact me as soon as he returns to the vehicle. 10-4?" Randy responded and said, "10-4! Over and out." The radio went silent and then the dispatcher said, "Over and out?"

At this point Randy was pulling through the gated community of Big Oak and about to cross onto Hibiscus Road. He faced about a 1 mile drive through a residential community to get to Vonn Road. Once on Vonn Road he knew he would go east and ride along the border of the North East Communications Network and Mid City Communications Networks service areas a substantial roaming zone. The upside of this was while he was in the roaming zone Game of Your Life players could not track him with any fluidity but the downside was the police could track him from a

# THE GAME OF YOUR LIFE

helicopter.

So Randy pulled over and got out and checked the roof of the car to see if its call numbers were written on the rooftop. And as expected they were. Now he knew he had to be even more careful and stay on as many tree lined streets as possible and as long as possible.

Just as Randy got back into the car and started off again, he heard a helicopter over head. He slowed down to get a good look and see if it was a police copter or a news/traffic chopper, them he heard the dispatcher say, "Patrol 456 this is dispatch do you copy?" Randy started to panic again but he waited. The dispatcher called again and said, "Patrol 456 come in." Again Randy was silent but he continued to drive towards Vonn Road staying under the tree line.

Finally the dispatcher said, "I don't know who you are driving that patrol car but right now you are merely in violation and subject to a misdemeanor for operating a police vehicle without permission. Pull over and step out of the vehicle with your hands up and no further offenses will be charged against you, but you must pull over right now."

Then the radio went silent again, and Randy floored the

# THE GAME OF YOUR LIFE

gas peddle. He quickly went from 30 miles per hour to 80 miles an hour in a residential zone.

The dispatcher immediately called back and said, "I repeat if you pull over now you will only face a misdemeanor vehicle offense that might only require a fine. But you must pull over right now." Randy pulled into a townhouse complex and started to speed through the various parking lots, dodging cars and pedestrians all at the same time. Finally he put on the lights and sirens and it forced more people to pay attention and move out of the way quicker but he could still hear the helicopter following him.

With the helicopter hovering overhead Randy knew he couldn't get away so he looked for an above ground parking garage. He knew there was one about a mile from Vonn Road in an adjoining apartment complex and he headed right for it. As Randy approached a road block about three blocks ahead he made a hard right turn and drove right into a private pay above ground parking lot. Crashing through their turnstile and skidding to an immediate stop in front of the garage attendant. The parking lot attendant who was almost ran over regained his composure and stepped out of his booth towards Randy. Randy turned off the siren and held up his wallet and yelled, "Where did that last car

# THE GAME OF YOUR LIFE

park?" the attendant said, "Up on the top floor where they usually park, that was Mr. Owens' car." Randy opened the rear car door and pulled out his bike and said, "Don't let any one in until I tell you to!" Then he rode off towards the upstairs ramp. The attendant said, "Yes Sir" and went to lock the facility down. Randy rode his bike through to the far side of the 4 story lot just out of the attendants line of sight and then walked it out side around the back to the front of the lot where he had just driven into. He stood on the side of the parking lot entrance and watched a parade of police cars and parking tenants back up behind the Crown Vic he left in the entranceway.

Now as he just stands out side the parking lot and waits, and waits and waits. And finally there were over 10 private passenger cars plus 6 police cars backed up in the street during the late morning rush hour with the helicopter hovering over head.

Finally exactly what Randy had hoped for happened, one of the traffic jam victims became so irate that he got out of his car, left the drivers door open and the car running and walked to the front of the line to see what was going on. When he got out and looked around, noting that there were two cars behind him he calmly started his trek towards the parking lot attendant's

# THE GAME OF YOUR LIFE

booth some 12 cars away. That's when Randy sprang into action. Randy chained his bike to a tree and ran up from behind the last two blocked drivers and waved them to back up and away, telling them he was trying to get through to his car because his wife was about to give birth.

By the time the angry driver had gotten to the parking lot attendants booth Randy was in his car backing down the street out of the traffic jam.

When the police finished interviewing the parking lot attendant and broke up the traffic jam which grow to some 20 cars long in the meantime, Randy had calmly driven around the block and made the trek over to Vonn Road. The trip up Vonn was smooth.

Once Randy crossed into the U.S.A. Communications Network service area which circled across the other two networks service areas, he only had to stay in the roaming zone for another 1 mile before he reached Boyette Circle. Knowing that, that angry driver at the parking lot was probably blistering hot when he found out that his car was stolen and the cops would be just as hot over being tricked by some unknown car theft, Randy realized it was only going to be a matter of time before the police tracked him down in that car. So

# THE GAME OF YOUR LIFE

Randy decided he would dump the car he was driving and take the B4 bus on 126$^{th}$ Ave., to throw the cops off his trail.

Once Randy got to Boyette Circle he parked the car and left the drivers side door partially opened, hoping that some real life car theft would pick it up and finish leading the cops astray. He walked over to 130th St. and catch the Mid City Bus number B4. The plan was to take the mile and a half ride to 128th Ave. and Jackson St.

With sunglasses on, and his afro wig under his New York Mets baseball cap Randy walked the block an a half to 130$^{th}$ St. and patiently waited for the 'B-4' bus to arrive. When the bus finally pulled up and the door opened the driver looked so hard at Randy; Randy thought the man was going to look through him. Randy swiped his debit card and went to his seat. But before the driver pulled off he checked the name on the debit card and then watched Randy walk to his seat.

There were only a few students on the bus then and once the bus dropped them off at 129$^{th}$ St. the bus was empty except for Randy and the driver. When the driver pulled off from the 129$^{th}$ St. stop randy could see the driver looking in his rear view mirror at him. When the

# THE GAME OF YOUR LIFE

driver realized Randy was watching him, watching him
he said, "Hey buddy you going over to the Global
Building? If so this is the wrong bus." Randy paused
for a second and then looked around and said, "You
talking to me?" The driver smiled and said, "I ain't
talking to myself. I said, you going over to the Global
Building?" Randy said, "No, no I'm on my way to 128$^{th}$
St. to do some shopping."

The driver pulled off and slowly pulled into traffic.
Then he looked up in the rear view mirror again and
smiled and said, "Your name Randy?"

Randy now realized that the bus driver had recognized
his face and gotten his name from his debit card. So
now he knows who Randy was and what he was about
to do. So Randy stood up and said, "I'm good you can
let me off at the next stop." The bus driver then said,
"Oh you got a few stops to go, relax. I got you." Randy
walked to the rear door and pushed the door bell. The
driver said, "Don't worry I'll get you to 128$^{th}$ St. it's
right up the avenue here. It will only be a minute,
relax." Randy stood there for another minute and then
he rang the bell again as the bus passed the 129$^{th}$ St.
stop. Then Randy said, "Look I asked to get off at that
stop. It's your job to respond to my directions." The
Bus driver smiled and started texting something on his

# THE GAME OF YOUR LIFE

phone while he drove. Then he said, "What's the hurry Mr. Hatchfield? Getting all excited about claiming your big money today? Don't worry I'll get you to the claims office on time."

Now Randy knew exactly what was happening, this guy was holding him hostage until he could meet up with his co-hi-jacker. Then Randy knew he wouldn't have a chance. So Randy said, "Look I know what you are thinking and you're a City employee ineligible to collect or participate in any games of chance."

The driver now watching for his cohort and watching Randy standing at the rear door, said, "Who me, participate in any thing that would jeopardize my pension? No way. Besides there is less hassle and profit when you let your fingers do the talking. Your escorts are right up here."

Randy could see two rather large dark haired men all dressed in black and standing at the next bus stop. One standing where the front door would open and the other standing where the rear door would open.

Randy quickly reached in his backpack and pulled out his taser and his ice pick. When the bus stopped and the bus driver only opened the front door, letting the larger

# THE GAME OF YOUR LIFE

of the two men on first. As the big guy walked towards Randy the bus driver said, "I calculate he should have about $15,000 in Claims receipts and accumulated bonus dollars of $500,000 give or take. And tell Ralphie not to forget my share this time. I always do the right thing, you know." By now the rear door was opening and Randy barely had enough time to jump up in the rear door well and kick the man coming in the rear door in the chest. As Randy came down outside of the bus he pointed back behind him and tased the larger guy in the neck sending him jerking and kicking like a chicken with its head cut off, with that he ran off. Randy had to leave the taser behind. Then the guy who Randy kicked in the chest, stumbled around for a moment and finally composed himself then began to run after him. The chase lasted about a half a block before the big guy ran out of wind.

Randy ran around the corner and up the side street until he saw a cab dropping off a couple of passengers. Randy hoped in the back seat and said, "I'm late for an interview can you take me up to Jackson St. over by 128th Ave. and 125th St. you know the Helm Ave. junction, as fast as you can?"

The cab driver a small Indian man responded by immediately locking the doors and then speaking with a

# THE GAME OF YOUR LIFE

heavy accent said, "This is my lucky day. Thank Ali it is my lucky day. All thanks to Ali." Randy did not respond but pulled off his backpack and slide over into the middle of the back seat where the driver could see him. Then Randy pulled out some black masking tape showed that to the driver, pulled out his book of matches and showed that to the driver. The driver now trying to speed up, was distracted between watching traffic and what Randy was doing, had difficulty trying to call his co-hi-jacking partner. Then Randy taped 2 of his M-80's to the rear window of the car so the driver could see it.

The driver smiled and said, "That will not hurt me. You can't stop this car with that, my friend. I thanked Ali for this good fortune already so I am protected from your devises."

Randy ducked down, covered his ears and lit the match and then lit the wick. About four seconds went by and the driver was in the middle of saying, 'I told you Ali would protect me'…, when the M-80's went off. All of the windows in every car within a 30 foot circumference blow out including the cab driver's rear seat protective window, his front windshield and all of his side door windows. The car engine stalled and the automatic burglar alarm went off. In the chaos Randy

# THE GAME OF YOUR LIFE

crawled out of the rear window and ran off towards the Helm Ave. junction.

When Randy arrived at the junction he quickly slipped down a subway stairwell for the Mid City Transit Line, onto the North 134th Ave and Ulmerton Road platform heading towards 120th St. and Ridgecrest Park.

Randy knew he could pick up a bike in the park and ride it back to 134th Ave. and 121st St.  Once there he planned to use his inline Rollerblades to skate the final half mile from 121st St. to the 3500 block on 134th Ave. the entrance to the Global Video Game Development Claims Office complex, where the final test would begin.

# THE GAME OF YOUR LIFE

## CHAPTER 5

# FATAL ATTRACTION

Standing outside the subway entrance was Lisa Barnett, a tall slender full breasted 30 year old Ethiopian hair dresser and part time bartender at the Pink Kitty Cat Club just across from the Global Video Game complex.

She followed Randy down the stairwell and as he stood on the subway platform and picked his backpack pockets. When Randy noticed how close she was standing he moved a few feet away. Within a minute she was back up under him, picking his backpack pocket again. The first thing she took was one of his 2 remaining M-80 firecrackers. Next she took one of his two tazers. But before she could take anything else Randy grabbed her around the neck and shoved her up against a wall.

Lisa put on a terrified look and started to scream but Randy was holding her throat so tight she could hardly breathe. Then she tried to knee him in the groan and missed because Randy was standing arms length away

# THE GAME OF YOUR LIFE

from her. Finally she gave up and mouthed, 'what do you want?'

Randy loosened his grip and said, "… everything you took out of my backpack." Lisa tried to put on a big bright smile and show all 32 teeth but Randy's grip tightened up again, so she reached in her back pocket and pulled out the M-80 and gave it to him.

By now the train was pulling into the station and a crowd of people started to get on the train. Randy let her go and walked towards the train. He got as close to the rear exit door as he could, he had hoped to put his back against the train wall and stand perfectly still the entire ride so he wouldn't be noticed. But a group of young Evangelist came walking through the car, asking for offerings and handing out tracks.

There were about 8 of them all wearing white t-shirts with the logo 'Lord Do It 4Me' on the front and back, with black pants and black converse sneakers.

When the leader, a tall muscular black men, saw Randy standing over against the train car rear door wall he walked over and said, "Hey! Hey you! Care to make an offering?" Randy looked up at him and slowly pulled off his backpack and rifled through it for his money. As

# THE GAME OF YOUR LIFE

he did he realized that the young woman who had just picked his pocket was standing next to him again and still smiling. Randy felt around in his backpack and the woman started to walk away. Randy quickly grabbed the top two bills in his pocket and handed them to the young man and went after the woman. The young man thanked Randy and then looked at what Randy had handed him, saw it was two $100 bills and then he went to personally thank him. That was the most money anyone had ever given at one time.

As Randy quickly followed the woman to the other end of the subway car, the train came to a stop and people started getting on and off. Finally when the car doors closed and the train took off again Randy saw the woman walking through the front car door to the next car. Randy moved as fast as he could and caught up with her in the next car.

He grabbed her by the arm and pulled her back toward him. As she stumbled back she caught the eye of a young Hispanic man and made a kissing gesture at him and mouths the words 'help me'.

The young Hispanic man and his four friends walked over to Randy and the woman and asked what was going on. Randy said, "Nothing." Lisa said, "Why don't you mind your own business?" To the Hispanic man. Then she started acting as if she was totally in love with Randy, kissing all over him and calling him honey and asking him to take her away from these fresh men.

Randy was totally confused but he remained focused and started to search her pants pockets as she cuddled all over him. By the time Randy found his tasers in her back pocket the Hispanic man had become more confused and now irate. He began cursing and yelling back at Lisa. She then became agitated and yelled at Randy to put him in his place.

Just as Randy finished retrieving his property the Hispanic man, grabbed him and pulled him away from Lisa. Another Hispanic man, who was with him, pulled out a knife and a third man showed his handgun which was in his waist band. The forth man grabbed Randy from behind and held him in a bear hug. Then the first Hispanic man started pointing and yelling at Randy and Lisa and was preparing to swing and hit Randy.

That is when the big black guy from the first car entered and grabbed the first Hispanic man's arm. He looked at the other three men as he lifted their leader off the floor and said, "Before I break this arm off, you thinking about getting some too?" Then the other 7

# THE GAME OF YOUR LIFE

members of the black man's group made themselves apparent, by showing their machetes and handguns as well.

The young Hispanic man who had been lifted off the floor started screaming "No Mass, no mass." The train came to a sudden stop because someone pulled the emergency cord. Every one was jostled against everyone else and the big guy let the young Hispanic guy loose. The train doors sprung open and people started running every which way. Then the big black guy looked at Randy, smiled and said, "Thanks for the offering, may God Bless you and yours." He nodded his head goodbye and got off the train with the others in his group right behind the group of young Hispanic men.

Randy waved goodbye and said, "No problem and thank you." Then Randy grabbed Lisa by the arm again and said, "You stand right here while I double check if I got all of my things back."

Lisa smiled and said, "I like you. Do you like me?" Randy looked at her and said, "You like me? You got a funny way of introducing yourself, has anybody ever told you that?"

Lisa smiled again and said, "Not really, why do you say

# THE GAME OF YOUR LIFE

that?" Randy looking confused said, "So do you clip every man you like?" as he put his backpack on. Then he said, "What else did you take?" Lisa said, "Are we going to see each other again?" Randy smiled and said, "While I might be crazy to say this; I guess not. Not unless we are naked on the beach so I don't have to worry about you clipping me again." Lisa smiled and said, "I can go for that. I think you are nice and good looking. You don't think I am nice? I gave you back all of your stuff. I was just playing with you. I actually know who you are too."

Randy said, "Yeah I am sure you know who I am, you probably took my wallet and touch phone while I wasn't looking as well."

Lisa smiled and said, "I gave you back all of your toys, don't be mad, big daddy!"

Right then Randy realized that this woman was going to be hard to forget.

The train stopped and Randy got off and started to walk up the stairwell to the street. Lisa followed him begging him to wait up for her. Now at North 134th Ave and Ulmerton Road, Randy just needed to slip into Ridgecrest Park and walk along the bike path until he

# THE GAME OF YOUR LIFE

found an unattended bike. The problem was dumping Lisa without letting her know where he was going, and without closing the now open door to see her again, if he reconsiders later.

As Randy walked along the tree-lined bike path Lisa continued trying to engage him in conversation. She had already poured out her life story and was now trying to coaxes Randy into letting his inner man come out.

Within the first 50 yards on the bike path, Randy spotted a nice 15 speed bike unattended. But Lisa rambled on so loud it brought the owner back out from behind the bushes with his date to check on his bike.

Randy decided he had to dump Lisa right away if he was to keep his timetable. So Randy stopped and sat on a bench then asked Lisa to come and sit next to him, immediately she overreacted and cuddled up right under his arm.

Randy accepted her advance out of pure exhaustion and then said, "Why me? Of all the men in this city? Why would a pretty young woman like you find me so attractive?" Lisa looked up into his eyes and smiled and said, "Because you are you, that's why! I liked you the

# THE GAME OF YOUR LIFE

moment I saw you. My blood just ran hot and I just knew you were someone for me."

Randy sighed and said, "That sounds nice, but really, why me?"

Lisa sighed, sat up, and looked him in the eyes and said, "Do you really want the truth? I mean the God's honest truth? Now don't get mad, but hear me out first. Ok?"

Randy looked back at her and said, "Ok! I'll listen first."

Lisa started to well up and a tear appeared in her eye when she said, "I have been watching you for several months now, along with three other Video Game players. It's like my job you know. Although I have not signed up to become a Quality Assurance agent. My boyfriend gives me money to track people online. He's a cop. And what we do is, when we find a big money claimer he helps them get into the Claims Clerks office because of his job and then we split the winnings. He is planning on leaving the police force to do this full time but he wants to have a nice nest egg to carry us. My problem is I am afraid to leave him right now. I was hoping that if we made a big score he would have enough money that he would leave me and find

85

# THE GAME OF YOUR LIFE

someone else."

Then Randy said, "Wow! So are you looking to help me get into the Claims Clerks office for a split of my claim?"

Lisa shrugged her shoulders and said, "I don't know what to do now. I couldn't keep hanging around you and not tell you the truth and now I'm gonna have to go back to Jake and explain what I did. But I just can't tell him how I feel about you or use to feel about him. I don't know what to do." And she started to sob.

Randy said, "So how does this work? How does he get people into the Claims office without them realizing what he is doing?"

Lisa said, "Well when people become unruly outside the Claims Office they sometimes call the police. When the police come they have to find out if the company wants to file charges. So the cops come in and go up to the penthouse and speak to the VP in charge first, to identify the person or persons. Then they go back downstairs get the person bring them back to the penthouse for positive I.D. and take a formal statement charging them with whatever crime. Then they take them out in handcuffs.

# THE GAME OF YOUR LIFE

But sometimes when Jake and his partner bring the person up, they get away from them and run into the Claims Clerks office. They collect their payment and when they come out, Jake and his partner take their share and then they just wind up taking the person to the precinct where they wind up paying their fine for whatever charge they have. And then they go home, with whatever they have left over, I guess."

Randy said, "Wow! So what were you supposed to do with me? Explain how this whole day was supposed to work out."

Lisa said, "Why? You already know how I feel about you, and what the plan was." Randy said, "I might be interested in going along, you know, splitting with you guys so that it is easier. Easy money is always better than hard earned money you know." They both busted out laughing. Then Lisa said, "But what about us? You think you would like to get to know me?"

Randy, pulled her close and kissed her and kissed her again and then she kissed him hard.

Then he smiled and said, "Trust me, I really want to get to know you better on more than one level."

# THE GAME OF YOUR LIFE

Lisa said, "Good, now I'm happy. Ok, now as for your question; I will text Jake and tell him what time you will be downstairs on line. I am supposed to go and watch your back and hopefully you make it inside. If not he will come and bust you for some reason and then take you inside and upstairs. When they pay you, you are to request 2 cash cards. Give one to me and everything is good. But let me tell you right now, if you try to stiff him, he will become very angry and get revenge. I have never seen him get angry but I can tell you from experience all of those who have tried to stiff him I have yet to see any of them again, so whatever."

Randy said, "Well I don't see any reason to stiff you guy's, you are doing me a big favor and making my effort easier. And I know that there is enough to go around…so you can tell him I'm good with it. Right now it is about 2:00pm I should be at the Claims Office complex in about two hours. Let me know if that works for him." Lisa smiled and said, "you sure two hours is enough time, big daddy?"

Randy smiled and said, "Not for you and me, but business before pleasure, always."

Lisa said, "Good then we will have more time to

# THE GAME OF YOUR LIFE

explore each other later. I'm gonna tell Jake that it is over as soon as you give him his share. I have enough money to carry me for a while and we can see where it goes with us."

When Lisa finished texting Jake both her and Randy started back through the park looking for a couple of bikes to borrow to finish the journey to the Claims Clerks office. While they were strolling along the bike path Lisa asked Randy what his plan of approach to the claims clerks office was going to be. And Randy explained that he planned to get a bike and ride it back to 134th Ave. and 121st St. and then make his way over the final half mile to 3500 134th Ave. on foot.

At that moment Randy was still conflicted about the timing and sincerity of Lisa and her feelings for him. Randy figured he needed to continue to go along but play things close to the vest and worst case he could use a surprise sacrificial decoy once he arrived at the Claims Clerks office.

When Lisa thought about the route Randy was taking she said, "Doesn't that route take you past the Claims Clerks office by almost a half mile?"

Randy responded and said, "Does it?" Then he saw the

# THE GAME OF YOUR LIFE

hot dog vendors cart in the clearing and he said, "Let's stop over there at the street vendors wagon and get something to eat then we can go over my map." She agreed and they walked over towards the hot dog wagon to get something to eat.

Now walking like a couple of sweethearts, holding hands and looking into each others eyes they didn't notice the crowd of motorcycle riders forming behind the hot dog vendors wagon near the bath houses and pool area about 20 yards away from the vendors cart.

By the time Randy and Lisa got close enough to seriously start thinking about what they would buy, a couple of the bikers had walked up to the hot dog vendor and started to place their orders.

Thankfully a team of cops also pulled up and parked a few yards away from where the bikers were gathering, but closer to where the bikers were than the hot dog vendor's stand. As soon as Randy and Lisa walked up and got the vendors attention one of the biker's recognized Randy from his iphone video stream and said, "Randy! Hey Randy Hatchfield! That you?"

Randy was again caught off guard so he had to improvise and he said, "Who wants to know?" this

# THE GAME OF YOUR LIFE

confident voice threw the biker for a second, and he looked at Randy and then looked back at his partner and said, "That's Randy Hatchfield, man he's worth a lot of money in this 'Game of Your Life' reality show! Let's get him and take his voucher receipts, man."

Then the two men started to step towards Randy while pulling their guns out. The first man walked right up to Randy and pointed his gun at his head, smiled and said, "Hand over those voucher receipts or I'll blow your head off and take them. Then maybe I'll do your little lady friend right here just for fun."

The second man went to step up behind him but he noticed the police officers jumping out of their car and pulling there guns as they ran towards them.

The second biker said, "Frank! Man are you crazy? The cops are coming, get it or quit it man we got to go!" The first biker said, "What no response? Well I guess it's decided…" And Lisa hit him with Randy's stun gun in the arm, the jerking of his body resulted in his gun firing and the bullet striking Lisa in the head. As she fell backward the second biker turned and fired at the cops who stopped, dropped and returned fire killing him and the hot dog vendor. Randy ducked and slipped behind the hot dog stand. As everyone in the area

# THE GAME OF YOUR LIFE

started screaming and running every which way. All of the bikers revved up their bikes with a loud roar and started to take off in a cloud of dust. Then the police officers cautiously approached and checked the three bodies. By now Randy had slipped off into the stampeding crowd. He found a bike and sped off towards the 134$^{th}$ Ave. and 121$^{st}$ Street exit.

When he got to the corner of 134$^{th}$ Ave. and 121$^{st}$ St he dumped the bike in the bushes and put on his roller-skates.

It took almost an hour to skate the remaining 10 blocks to the Global Video Developers office complex because Randy would skate up a block, cross the street, skate back down the block, then cross the street again and skate back up 2 blocks and start all over again.

The stretch of road Randy rambled along was inside a roaming zone and he figured if there was a 3 minute disconnect in service, anyone watching him would not be able to figure out if he was traveling to the complex or whether there was a break in the video stream.

Global Video Game Developers Corporate Complex Lobby Area

# THE GAME OF YOUR LIFE

Officer's Thomas and Ore had arrived at 3:00pm along with the investigating detective in charge of the day's earlier rooftop jumping incident, to further examine the security tapes and re-interview all personnel who may have seen the victims.

Just as Ofc. Ore got out of their new patrol car a message came over the car radio. Alerting all cars to be on the look out for any of the Mid City Phantoms Motorcycle Clubs members. They were wanted for questioning in a public execution of two Ridgecrest Park patrons. A registered park vendor named Giuseppe De Costa and a female park visitor by the name of Lisa Felema where gunned down and killed…

When Ofc. Jake Thomas heard Lisa's name he almost fainted. He became visibly shaken and sick to his stomach. Ofc. Ore saw him struggling to maintain his composure and asked if everything was alright, Ofc. Thomas just shook his head and said, he was alright. Then he said he hit his funny bone getting out of the car but he would be alright.

Now all Ofc. Thomas could think about was that Randy Hatchfield was somehow responsible for Lisa's death and he wanted to find him and make him pay.

# THE GAME OF YOUR LIFE

The law enforcement trio entered the lobby and informed the security guard that they were there concerning the jumpers, and he contacted the corporate office to have the executive authorize their entry.

VP Thom Gullota and his intern Bill Mahner came down and escorted the trio back up to the rooftop crime scene. Lead Investigating Detective Harry Brown took a walk around the rooftop and then proceeded to inquire of the executives how this tragedy could have occurred.

Det. Brown asked Mr. Gullota how could anyone gain access to the roof? Mr. Gullota looked around and said, "There are two entrance points on the roof." He went on to say the access points allow for free access but exiting or reentry can only be accomplished with an electronic or digital key card. Of course if they decided to repel off of the roof top that is an option but I for one couldn't begin to phantom that. However we do have substantial financial resources on the floor below, such as credit cards, cash cards and debit cards. We like to be prepared to accommodate our voucher payment recipients any way they feel comfortable, you know?"

Det. Brown went over and examined the rooftop entrance doors and said, "These doors lock from the inside only?" Mr. Gullota said, "Yes, unobstructed

# THE GAME OF YOUR LIFE

access is only outward to the roof, to return you must have a key card." Det. Brown then said, "Oh! Yeah! You just said that. Question are those security camera's operable?" Mr. Gullota smiled and said, "24 hours a day, 7 days a week."

Det. Brown then said, "Well who was monitoring those sight lines this morning?"

Mr. Gullota looked at Bill Mahner and then back at Det. Brown and said, "The security detail, I suppose!" Det. Brown smiled and said, "Would you give us access to the guard and the video files?" Mr. Gullota said, "Of course, right this way, gentlemen." And the men went back inside, and down the roof access stairwell to the penthouse office suite elevator. As the men got on the elevator to go down to the security control center on the second floor, Det. Brown said, "I see there is no direct elevator acccss to the roof top but is there a service elevator to the penthouse?" Mr. Gullota said, "Absolutely not detective." Then Det. Brown turned around and said, "So where does that door lead too?"

Mr. Gullota looked and then said, "Oh! Right! That is the janitors dumb waiter. We only use that for moving supplies, furniture and rubbish, you know. Why?" Det. Brown said, "Does it access the roof?" Mr. Gullota looked down at the floor and said, "Unfortunately detective it does. I apologize. I rarely notice it and forgot to mention it. Please forgive me."

Det. Brown then said, "Not a problem, but I have to ask, is that dumb waiter also monitored by the security system?" Mr. Gullota said, "I am sorry to say detective but I really can't answer that question because I really don't know. I guess we'll just have to find out when we get down to the security office." Det. Brown walked back to the dumbwaiter door and opened it. The dumbwaiter was of good size almost a 6' x 6' square and about 9' high. It was clean and had no visible security camera's inside or directly pointing to it from the lobby area.

Det. Brown finished his inspection and returned to the penthouse elevator and the men went down to the security control room on the second floor.
Complex Security Control Center 2$^{nd}$ Floor

Inside the security control center Det. Brown found out that all of the surveillance cameras feed into two different recording consoles, one for interior activity and the other for exterior activities.

Det. Brown asked Ofc. Ore to review the interior feeds

# THE GAME OF YOUR LIFE

while Ofc. Thomas reviewed the exterior feeds and he would continue his interviews of the onsite personnel.

About an hour later both Ofc's had found, cued up some clips of interest and asked Det. Brown to return to the control room to go over the clips. While they waited for Det. Brown to return, the officers quietly talked.

Ofc. Ore asked Ofc. Thomas if there were any referrals expected for the day. Ofc. Thomas said, "Yeah there is one but this one is the tri-fecta. Lisa was bringing him here just before she got shot. And get this, it was the same guy who clipped our patrol car this morning, Randy Hatchfield. The guy everyone is looking for, for the murder of that postal worker this morning." Ofc. Ore then said, "So what are you thinking?" Ofc. Thomas responded, "Look; Lisa was a snitch but she was great in bed, she scoped out a lot of Claimers for us so we owe her. I say when this guy shows up let's just take him out in cuffs, take him for a ride and rid the world of the likes of him, and then we can find some stooge to present his claims later on tonight." Then Ofc. Ore said, "So what are the numbers like?" Ofc. Thomas replied, "We're looking at about half a mil when you add in the bonus money."

Ofc. Ore said, "Sweet. What time is he expected?" Ofc.

# THE GAME OF YOUR LIFE

Thomas said, "He should be here any minute now." Then Ofc. Ore said, "So how do you want to handle it. Det. Brown is straight laced and he ain't gonna over look this." Ofc. Thomas said, "Look we have all the pieces in place, Hatchfield is a fugitive looking at a felony charge at worst and at best he is wanted on a misdemeanor warrant for operating a police vehicle without permission. All we need to do is pick him up before someone else does. Det. Brown can get anybody to help in his investigation." Then Ofc. Ore said, "Sounds like a plan to me, Rookie."

Then Ofc. Ore asked, "What did you see on those video tapes, anything interesting?"

Ofc. Thomas responded, "I saw the Janitor leave the dumbwaiter door wedged open with his cleaning cart to go get something and those three jumpers slipped in and took the elevator up to the roof."

Ofc. Ore then said, "Yeah, yeah! I saw them come out onto the roof and it looked like the access door slammed closed behind them. Then they got to arguing for a while and finally it looked like they thought they could repel over the side of the roof and use their weigh to break through the outside office window of the clerks office to gain entry." Ofc. Thomas said, "What were

# THE GAME OF YOUR LIFE

they going to use to repel with?" Ofc. Ore responded and said, "They latched their belts together." The men both busted out laughing as Det. Brown walked in and said, "What's so funny?"

# THE GAME OF YOUR LIFE

## CHAPTER 6

# TO THE PENTHOUSE

4:00PM Outside Global Video Game Developers Complex

Carrying his "Protest sign," Randy walked through the parking lot directly towards the entrance for the Claims Clerks office. As usual there was a crowd of potential claim hi-jackers and video game protesters in general, surrounding the entranceway.

Randy used his protest poster to obscure his face as best he could. His plan was to get on line and wait his turn to enter the Claims Clerks Office access lobby. Once at the entrance door, where the security guard is usually overwhelmed sorting the protesters from the Claimers, and the Hi-Jackers from the Claimers. Randy planned to slip into the lobby while the security guard is distracted with some other entrant, through the exit door which stands next to the entrance door, and get to the service elevator.

# THE GAME OF YOUR LIFE

The best way Randy could figure to get by the security guard was to start a panic which would cause a surge in the approaching line of some two to three hundred people. The chaos would be distraction enough, if he was in the right place to take advantage of the momentum and slip in through the exit door.

As Randy approached the entrance doorway, holding his sign in front of his face, he pulled out a M-80 firecracker, lit it and throw it towards the rear of the line. When it went off, with a loud blast, everyone pushed forward. The force of the crowd leaning and pushing forward was enough to break the double pane glass door windows in front of the security guards desk. The security guard immediately pulled his weapon and locked down the access elevator, then he called for back up.

The high volume outdoor alarm went off and within seconds there were 40 security guards running every way possible. Between the screaming and the yelling Randy managed to move even closer to the entryway. Then Randy lit his last M-80 and throw it at the rear of the line again and sheer pandemonium broke out with people not only pushing to gain access to the building but people just running for cover.

# THE GAME OF YOUR LIFE

While people pushed and shoved Randy throw a handful of dollar bills to the right of the entryway and utter chaos broke out with people grabbing and fighting for the bills.

That was when Randy made his move to slip inside. He ducked down behind the people in the front of the line and pushed his way through the crowd managing to just slip inside the front doorway; while the security guard was literally hemmed up by several Claim filers, Randy was able handcuff both the front entrance door handle to the front exit door handle, virtually locking everyone else out except for the ones who were struggling with the security guards. Then Randy ran to the service elevator which was clearly marked.

Once inside he realized that the service elevator did not access the penthouse floor but it did access the floor below it.

Randy made it to the $32^{nd}$ floor, got off the elevator and made his way to the stairwell which only lead to the rooftop, without allowing for access to the penthouse floor. That forced him to return to the $32^{nd}$ floor lobby where he saw the janitor pushing his cart into the rubbish dumbwaiter.

# THE GAME OF YOUR LIFE

Randy ran down the hallway towards the dumbwaiter and just made it inside, behind the then startled the janitor.

Looking up from behind the cleaning cart the janitor said, "Hello, how are you?" Randy said, "I'm in a hurry I need to get to the Claims Clerks office." The janitor said, "I'm going up there right now, too. But; you are not allowed to access the Claims Clerks office on the dumbwaiter you are supposed to access the penthouse floor from the regular elevator bank."

Randy said, "Does this elevator empty out into the penthouse lobby?" The janitor said, "Yes, it does."

Then Randy said, "Then it will have to do, could you push the button?"

The janitor said, "My name is William, William Stone. What is your name?"

Randy said, "Does it really matter?" As William pushed the button to go up and the doors closed he said, "No! Not really." Then just as the doors shut William reached down and grabbed the guide rail on the cleaning cart and pushed it up against Randy's stomach and pinned him against the door. He braced himself there holding Randy at bay while he pulled out a gas mask. Then he put it on and pulled out an aerosol canister and set it off. The elevator quickly filled with a white smoke and Randy fell over, right into the cleaning carts trash bin. Then William pushed some rubbish and papers over Randy's body and after about a minute he pushed the button for the penthouse and the elevator took off.

Once the elevator reached the penthouse floor William emerged dressed in Randy's shirt and pants. He pushed the cleaning cart into the lobby area just outside of the receptionist view. Then with Randy's baseball cap pulled down close to his eyes, he greeted the receptionist and told her that he was Randy Hatchfield and that he was there to present his claims to the Claims Clerk, could he go in and she opened the door and let him in.

Just inside the Claims Clerks office stood Ofc's Thomas and Ore along with Det. Brown the Claims Clerk and Bill Mahner.

When the receptionist opened the door and introduced Randy Hatchfield the Ofc's turned around and draw their weapons. The receptionist immediately withdraw and closed the door. Then she ran to the bathroom.

# THE GAME OF YOUR LIFE

After a moment Ofc's Ore and Thomas followed by Det. Brown brought William out in handcuffs with a gag over his mouth. The men got on the elevator and left.

As the men walked out of the Claims Clerks office, both the Claims Clerk and Bill Mahner walked out to see the officers leave. Bill went to the restroom and the Claims Clerk walked back into his office. As the door closed behind him Randy slipped inside.

Randy presented his I.D. and told the Claims Clerk that he was robbed by the janitor and should still be permitted to collect on his voucher receipts as well as any bonus money he was entitled to. Bill Mahner returned and listened to what was going on. The Claims Clerk disagreed with Randy at first but when Randy reminded him that company employees were not entitled to make claims and since he could demonstrate that he was the rightful claimant he should be entitled to the money due.

Then Bill Mahner said, how are you going to prove you are the rightful claimant?" Randy said, "Because I know the claim receipt number." Bill then said if you can tell us the claim receipt number that Mr. Stone

# THE GAME OF YOUR LIFE

handed us, when he posed as you, we would have no choice but to consider you the rightful claimant.

Randy said, "The receipt number is 0123456789101112."

The Claims Clerk went to his computer and verified the receipt number and by the time Randy explained the day's activities as they corresponded to the other claims receipts William had submitted his total claim was for $750,000 in bonus dollars in addition to his claim for $74,400 for a total claim of $824,400.

# THE GAME OF YOUR LIFE
# Epilogue:

8:00AM The next morning in the Global Video Game
Developers lobby The Security Guards Post

The Security Guard was talking to the new janitor as he
signed in, about his predecessor who was arrested the
other evening for attempting to participate in the
company's reality game against policy. When he
finished he said, "Now Mr. Hatchfield take this
temporary access pass to the 33$^{rd}$ floor and ask for Mr.
Mahner he will assign you to your work station.
Welcome aboard and good luck…"

# THE GAME OF YOUR LIFE

## LIST OF OTHER TITLES BY THIS AUTHOR
## INCLUDING
## U.S. Marshal Harry Bailey, and the
## "The Parables of Life Series"

| Title | RELEASE DATES |
|---|---|
| 1- U.S. Marshal Harry Bailey and the case Of the Persistent Widow | February 2013 |
| 2- U.S. Marshal Harry Bailey and the case Of the Wicked Farmers | May 2013 |
| 3- U.S. Marshal Harry Bailey and the case Of the Minas | September 2013 |
| 4- U.S. Marshal Harry Bailey and the case Of the Hidden Treasure | December 2013 |
| 5- U.S. Marshal Harry Bailey and the case Of the Friend at Midnight | March 2014 |
| 6- U.S. Marshal Harry Bailey and the case Of the Foolish Virgins | June 2014 |
| 7- U.S. Marshal Harry Bailey and the case Of the Good Samaritan | December 2014 |
| 8- U.S. Marshal Harry Bailey and the case Of the Four Soils | May 2015 |
| 9- U.S. Marshal Harry Bailey and the case Of the Lost Coin | September 2015 |
| 10-U.S. Marshal Harry Bailey and the case Of the Prodigal Son | December 2015 |
| 11- U.S. Marshal Harry Bailey and the case Of the Two Debtors | March 2016 |
| 12- U.S. Marshal Harry Bailey and the case Of the Two Sons | September 2016 |

Ask about our SPECIAL EDITION of U.S. Marshal Harry Bailey and the case of the CORPORATE KILLINGS available now!
www.usmarshalharrybailey.com

Other titles: The Way Station, U.S. Marshal Harry Bailey and the Corporate Killings and The Game of Your Life, 2-1-1 Emergency, Clinical Trials, Criminal Mastermind, The Deadly Mailman, Beyond The Way Station, Part II—To Hell for the Holidays, and look out for the 6 volume series U.S. Marshal Harry Bailey and the "City of Prophesy" series coming in 2015.